Honeymoon With The Prince: A Royal Romance

Brill Harper

Published by Brill Harper, 2018.

This is a work of fiction. Similarities to real people, places, or events are entirely coincidental.

HONEYMOON WITH THE PRINCE: A ROYAL ROMANCE

First edition. June 7, 2018.

Copyright © 2018 Brill Harper.

ISBN: 979-8223282068

Written by Brill Harper.

About this Book

His mousy temptress is pure, innocent, and untouched. But not for long...

Markellan Bran, the brutishly handsome Prince of Kentigen, is used to taking what he wants, and what he wants from first sight is the plain, simple, and American Violet Havisham for his wife. He sees what most don't when he looks at her—a curvy angel hiding an inner vixen. One who's hot as sin and a woman complex and challenging enough to be his bride. He is confident that he can conquer anything—and Violet's heart is next.

Violet Havisham finds everything about the brash, nearly uncivilized prince unsettling. She's recently left the monastery and craves a quiet life. Falling for a devil of man like Prince Markellan would be a royal mistake. He's too big, too brutish, and too darkly sensual for her. He says he wants to give her the one thing she left the cloister for—a baby. But surely she'd be better off adopting than taking her chances with a reckless, dangerous beast.

In his culture, the honeymoon comes before the wedding, and the bridegroom must convince the bride to marry him based on his honeymoon "performance." So Prince Markellan makes her a deal—give him one week to satisfy her every need, and if she can walk away, he'll let her go.

Author confession: If she can walk at all after a week in his palace, it will be a miracle. If you know what I mean. Did I mention that Prince Markellan's country is a fertility culture that worships women and all things carnal? The men there spend years learning the arts of pleasing and caring for their women. And you know he's not going to let her go with his royal baby in her belly. If you're looking for a curvy heroine, a royal hero, beastly alpha dirty talk, and opposites attract

in an instalove minute, you're in the right place. It wouldn't be a Brill Harper book if it wasn't as sweet as it is filthy.

Chapter One

Twenty years ago

Young Prince Markellan ran through the museum, ducking and weaving around the tourists. It was his first time in New York and no way was he hanging out in a stuffy old museum all day.

He was an adventurer.

Slipping past Ranzel had been too easy. See? He was made for this. He should have been born a pirate instead of a prince.

So what if he was only ten? Lots of pirates could have started as children. Argh.

He flew through a door marked *Employees Only* and found himself in a corridor. Yes! At the end was an exit to the street. He wanted to see Central Park so bad. He'd find it on his own. Run the whole way if he needed to. Nobody could stop him. Heck, maybe nobody would find him for days. He could eat...what did Americans call them? Hot dogs. For breakfast, lunch, and dinner. No, for dinner he'd eat cotton candy.

He was almost to the door when he heard the sound of a girl crying. He stopped and looked to his left to find a girl with long, blonde braids in a school uniform hugging her knees on the floor.

"Are you okay?" He dropped to the floor next to her. "Are you hurt somewhere?"

She snuffled and wiped her nose on her shirt. "I miss my mommy and daddy."

"Are you lost?" Shoot. He was wasting seconds he needed to put space between him and Ranzel, but he couldn't leave a crying, lost girl alone. His mother would skin him alive. The little girl was probably about three years younger than him. It was his duty to make sure she was okay.

"I'm not lost."

"Well, then, where are your parents?"

"God took them."

His heart fell. Oh, man. He understood that. "God took my dad too."

"What does he need them for? Doesn't he have enough people? Why can't he just take the old ones and leave the mommies and daddies here?"

He sat all the way down and crisscrossed his legs. This was going to take a while. "My mother told me that even though he isn't here where I can see him, my dad is always with me." And boy, is his dad probably mad right now. What was he thinking, running away from his guard? He was going to be in so much trouble. "Who are you here with?"

"My school. We're on a field trip. But I just got so sad and Sister Allison told me I need to be strong and not cry all the time, but I couldn't help it. The tears just started coming, so I ran to hide until the tears are gone."

Her eyes were all red and swollen, but they weren't leaking anymore. "Well, you should go back before you get into more trouble."

"What about you?"

"I guess I should go back too."

"My name is Violet."

"I'm Markellan." He dug into his pocket and pulled out the gold Kentigen medallion his father had given him a long time ago. He always had it in his pocket. Like a good luck charm. "Here."

"What is it?"

"So you remember when you're sad that you have a friend named Markellan."

She took it from him, and a little piece of his heart pinched when he parted with it. "Thank you. I'll keep it forever."

Sometimes, doing the right thing sucks.

"Let's get you back to your class."

He held her hand as they went back through the door he'd ducked through earlier. A mob of suits and even a couple of nuns rushed them, and he tried to keep hold of her hand as long as he could, but the grown-ups got them separated. He'd never forget her sad eyes, the color of the sky in June, when she looked back at him one last time.

Markellan

Current Day

"JUST ONE DRINK, PIETER."

"Your Majesty, it's too dangerous. You know that. We need advance warning to go into someplace like that. Have a drink in the suite."

I clench my fists. It isn't Pieter's fault that he is right, but I do not like rules for "my safety" as if I am a man who cannot take care of himself.

I have the same training as my royal guard. I pass all the same physical tests, the psychological ones too. If I were not of royal blood, I would be on an elite team myself.

Yet I cannot complain about being a prince. I am fortunate in my birth, and it's even better that I am the spare heir as I have no desire to rule.

But occasionally, I'd like to just be a normal man.

"Something less dangerous then," I say.

"Your Majesty..."

When the car stops, I unlock the door and ease out. "You may follow me at a safe distance, but I am taking a walk."

I don't wait for Pieter to acknowledge my order and begin walking down the street. I know he is behind me, and I can feel his curses as he flings them at my back. Poor Pieter. His father had been my guard in my childhood. Ranzel retired early because of me, I'm afraid. But Pieter is a good man, and one I enjoy drinking with. He's my best friend, though I'd never tell him that.

Ahead, I duck into a museum. I remember it from my first visit to New York when I was ten. The museum is quiet today. I stop at the ticket counter. "One adult, please."

"I'm sorry, sir, the museum is closing in ten minutes. It's too late to purchase entry." The blonde pushes my money back at me and gasps.

I am used to it. When someone recognizes me, it is either a gasp or a noise only a dog can hear.

She's a bit plain at first glance. A shapeless sweater covers her figure, but the swell of her breasts is unmistakable. I'm all about a nice set of tits, so I keep looking.

Her blonde hair is pulled into a ponytail at the nape of her neck. She's wearing round glasses and no makeup. A bit pudgy, but I am a lover of women of every size, so I decide to make her day. I open my mouth to say something charming that she will tell her friends about later, but the words get stuck in my throat.

Her eyes. They are familiar. How would I possibly know this woman? My heart picks up an unsteady pace, and it feels as if the ground is opening and I'm falling into it.

This sensation is new to me. I'm not one to get tongue-tied. It's just her eyes. They are so...blue.

It can't be. No way. What are the chances? It's been twenty years since I stepped foot in this museum.

"Violet?"

Chapter Two

Violet

I suck in a wet breath. Frozen.

The man is beautiful. Impossibly beautiful. Maybe even terrifyingly beautiful. I've never seen a man like him before. In real life, anyway. He's like my every darkest fantasy come to life. Fantasies I didn't even know I had. Fantasies I must have stuffed down tight, never to see the light of day until this moment.

He's definitely more than six feet tall. Powerfully built in a perfectly tailored suit meant to make him look civilized, but not doing its job very well. He's got firm, sensual lips on a savagely masculine face. A face shadowed with a dusting of a midnight black beard that matches the silky hair on his head.

That jaw. It's perfectly sculpted with a muscle leaping in it as he narrows his eyes.

My name. Did he really say my name?

How does this sinfully, sexy man with danger rolling off him know *my* name? I'm not wearing a name tag today.

My breath starts coming in shallow pants, and I look down. I don't have the skills for this man. I don't think any woman does. He's got to be a devil sent here to tempt us all right into his seductive trap.

"Violet? I can't believe you're really here. It's been twenty years. Did you never leave?" I look up, startled. He's smiling, but it makes me feel uneasy. It's a predator's smile, yet somehow familiar. "I used to wonder what happened to the little girl I met in the museum hall, but I never imagined she grew up in it. Do the exhibits come to life at night? Where do you sleep?"

He's teasing me. Most men don't even *see* me, and this darkly sensual man is teasing...wait. "Markellan?" The boy from the museum all those years ago?

My hand automatically goes to the round disc in the pocket of my cardigan. I'd made up wonderful stories about him, too. Ones just as fanciful as me living in a museum. In my imagination, he was a prince in the country of Kentigen, the name imprinted on the medallion he gave me all those years ago. My prince would come back and find me when he was old enough and whisk me away to his castle in the mountains. I'd become a princess and learn to ride horses and drink fancy tea and live happily ever after.

I imagined him handsome—in that sort of Prince Charming/Ken Doll way. Nothing like the gorgeous man in front of me. Oh, he is handsome—in an untamed barbarian sort of way. Like you know he's barely civilized no matter how finely tailored his suit is. My heart is hammering furiously, and heat lances me from head to toe; a kind of wild heat I've never felt before. I'm afraid I'm going to combust.

"I can't believe it's you," I whisper.

"I've been back to the city several times, but never here. I don't know what possessed me to come back today. Nostalgia, I guess. I always wondered what happened to the little girl with sad eyes."

Not much has happened. Not much at all.

"Well, I work here," I offer, ever the great conversationalist.

"Where we met."

"I can't even believe you remember me. Most people...don't."

A strange look passes over his face. "Of course I remember you. When I was a boy, I used to look up into the sky and wonder if you were looking up at the stars too." He clears his throat and loosens his collar as if he is uncomfortable with sentimentality.

"I did the same thing." Our gazes collide, and I have to dig deep for courage I don't feel. I can't let this opportunity pass me by. It won't come again. "I can't tell you how much it meant to me, your kindness that day.

It was such a painful part of my life, but I always remembered the way you took care of me when I was scared." I must be beet red right now. It feels like my skin is on fire. I pull out the medallion, rub the familiar raised marks on it. "Do you...do you want this back? I always wondered if you regretted giving it to a stranger that day. I know it meant a great deal to you."

I hold it out, and he stares at it like I'm holding a gun on him. "You still have it? You keep it with you?"

I nod. "Always."

He says nothing. Just stares at the golden medallion and then at me. Right at me. I don't think anyone has ever looked so closely at me before. Like I was a puzzle or a math problem to work out.

"Have dinner with me." It isn't a question or an offer. It is a command. From a man used to getting what he wants. A man so far out of my league he could be from Mars and have more in common with me than he does right now.

"I can't. I'm..." ...so very busy. Yes. I have the walk home to get to. The lonely dinner in my efficiency apartment. A book that waits for me to fall asleep reading. All so I can wake up and do the same thing tomorrow.

"Change your plans."

This time, his arrogant demand gets under my skin. My inner-spinster takes over and I purse my lips, even as I kick myself to stop acting so prudish. I will never get used to dealing with people normally, I'm afraid. "I'm sorry, but I can't." He hasn't taken the token out of my hand, so I slip it back into my pocket.

"Jealous boyfriend?" he asks.

I bristle. He must know I don't have a boyfriend, jealous or otherwise. I shake my head.

"Ah. You're afraid of me."

"Of course not." I'm so very afraid of him. He terrifies me. My skin feels like it's stretched too tightly over my bones, but I don't think that's fear. It's something new. A feeling I've never experienced before.

"I'm afraid I can't promise you that I don't bite. But I give you my word you won't complain," he tells me in that rock-tumbled voice. Gravel drug through honey. Dripping in honey.

The blood rushes too hard through my veins, and I feel woozy. "You shouldn't...talk like that."

"Does my flirting bother you?"

"Yes."

"Good. Have dinner with me."

"Why? What would we even talk about?"

The museum security guard comes by, eyeing up my late customer. "It's all clear," he tells me, meaning he's ready to lock the door behind me when I leave. I nod and grab my purse.

Markellan isn't taking the hint that it's closing time and I need to go. "We have twenty years of catching up to do. What *won't* we talk about?"

"I'm boring."

"Well, then I'll entertain you with my wild adventures. I don't just sneak around the back halls of museums, you know. I've upped my adventures over the years—I once stole my cousin's car and went for a joyride when I was thirteen. I'll tell you all about my childhood over the best steak in the city."

I shake my head. "You don't understand. I'm..."

"What? A nun?"

Oh, my face is absolutely on fire now.

A look of pure horror crosses his face as the realization dawns on him that he might have hit it in one. "No. No, you are not. Are you really a nun?"

I squeeze my eyes closed. It would be easier if I were. "Not exactly."

He huffs out a laugh. "I think that's one of those things like being a virgin. You are or you're not."

"I am...I mean I'm not...a nun. I was going to be a nun, but I left the convent."

He opens the swinging door of my desk area like a gentleman to let me out, yet I have a feeling it's all for show. He's no gentleman. I walk past him but turn quickly around, not trusting him at my back.

"So you're not a nun...but you are a virgin."

My mouth opens and closes like a fish gulping for air.

"You admitted it."

"I did no such thing!"

"Oh, so you're *not* a virgin?"

"Markellan! Have you no manners?"

He sends me a wolfish grin. "Not in abundance, my lamb, no."

The door dings, and I hear the guard mutter under his breath as two tall, muscular men rush in. "Your Majesty, we really must go."

"Your majesty?" I ask.

"Cancel my evening appointments. I'm having dinner with an old friend," he tells the man.

"Your majesty?" I ask again.

"Prince Markellan of Kentigen," he says with an indolent bow toward me. "At your service, my lady."

Chapter Three

Markellan

My lovely Violet has bewitched me.

I can think of no other reason that I'm suddenly obsessed with the perfect cupid bow of her sweet mouth.

Everything about her is lusciously plump, and I want nothing more than to taste every tantalizing inch of her body. I want to squeeze her delicate flesh. Mark her as mine.

We're in the limo, and I'm clenching my fists to keep from touching her. It's crazy. I know she thinks *I'm* crazy. I have no idea how I coaxed her into the car. Most women I've met would do backflips to get invited into my limousine, but not my lovely Violet. She looked at the driver holding the door for her as if he might be escorting her straight to hell. But in she went, finally. And now she's stark white and nervously chewing her lip.

I notice she's got my father's medallion in her hand, rubbing it mindlessly, and it fills me with a strange new emotion. That she's carried something of me with her all these years. That it comforts her.

She's bewitched me, I tell you.

She has none of the city polish I'm used to in this country. She's shy, yes, but there is an earthy quality to her that makes me want to just be near her. And the idea that she didn't even know who I was, didn't recognize me as a prince, intrigues me even more.

"I can't believe you're a prince."

"Some days I can scarcely believe it myself, lamb."

She shoots me a look that's meant to chastise but instead stirs my blood.

I don't know why she gasped at me earlier, if she didn't recognize me. I don't think I'll ask her just yet. She's...well, she's certainly bundled up tight, this one. Even her clothes. Her blouse goes up her neck to her chin, and she's holding her sweater together in one hand like the wind might blow it off her. "Why did you leave your convent?"

"I would have been a horrible nun."

Thank fuck. "But why did you leave?"

A smile, small and secret, changes her face completely. "I held a baby."

My mouth goes dry. It's like I can see right into her soul, the woman she hides, the woman she really is. And deep inside me, something awakens and roars. *Mine.* "A baby?"

She shakes her head a little, as if to clear a fog or talk herself out of something. "It's silly really."

My hand covers hers before I know I've done it. "Tell me."

"I'd never held one before. I don't know how to describe it, but I knew I could never choose a life that didn't allow for me to have one of my own. It was like this bone-deep knowing that I wanted to be a mother. I tried to push it away, but it was just so powerful. I knew I'd never be able to take the vows with my whole heart after that. It's ridiculous, really, since I have no more of a chance of having one now than I did as a nun."

"Why is that?" I ask, holding her hand more firmly. I can see her, in my bed, nursing my child in her arms. I can see it like it's a memory, it's so strong.

"I grew up in a convent orphanage. I spent my adult years until recently in preparation for a life in that same convent. I don't really understand the world of dating and marriage, and I have no idea how to get from the life I'm living to the one that I want." She stops and looks out the window, but I see her wipe away a tear she's trying to hide from me. "I can't believe I'm telling you this. You must be so bored."

I gently cup her face and bring her gaze back to mine. Those sweet, wet eyes take me back to that day when I was ten and knew I was to care for her. I guess that never went away.

I'm not a man who questions my impulses or spends time examining why I feel a certain way or why I want something that I covet. I have no intention of changing that now.

I push the intercom. "Get the jet ready. We're going home early."

"Yes, Your Majesty."

There are questions in her eyes.

"I'm not bored, lamb. In fact, you've inspired me."

"I see. If you'll just have your driver turn around, I can take the subway home, and you can get on your way."

"I have a different idea, Violet. You come to Kentigen with me." When I said we were going home, I meant she was coming home too. It's probably too early to tell her that.

"I can't go to Kentigen with you. I have a ..." The despair that crosses her face nearly undoes me.

I want to kiss her worries away. Promise her a new life. Fix everything that hurts. I've never been so inspired. But I know I will have to temper myself until she is used to me. Until she trusts me.

And then all bets are fucking off.

"What can't you leave behind?"

"I have a ...job. And an apartment. And..."

"Do you have a cat?"

She shakes her head. Confused. "No. Why?"

"Plants? Something in that apartment that needs you to care for it?"

She shudders on a breath. "No."

"Come with me to Kentigen. I will give you as many children as you desire to care for." She gasps, so I keep talking to prevent her arguments. "If your work at the museum is so important, I assure you there are artifacts and history needing preservation in my country that you can devote yourself to. Or charities. Or gardening. Anything you wish is yours."

"Markellan, what are you talking about? I can't go to Kentigen with you. This is ludicrous. You don't even know me." She pauses. "Did you say children? Do you want me to come back and be a nanny? I'm afraid that while I love children, I don't have much experience with them."

"I did say children. As many as you want." Her brow furrows. "I don't need a nanny yet. I need a wife."

"Are you saying..."

"Violet, I know no other way than to be blunt. I sense in you a woman who longs to break out. A woman who's lived a quiet life, a careful life, but hungers for more. I can give it to you. All that you desire. Come home with me. Be my bride, my princess. I will fill your belly full of royal babies, and you will never be lonely again."

"You're crazy. Please take me home. To my home. Or just...let me out. Here is fine."

I push down my irritation. Not at her. At myself. My mother would skin me alive if she saw how I was bungling this.

"I don't mean to frighten you. And I think if you search your heart right now, it's not me you're afraid of, but yourself."

I pull my phone out and dial my second guard, Con, putting him on speaker phone. "Con, you are from this moment on, attached to Violet. You are to protect her as you would me and make sure she gets what she needs and goes where she wants, even if it is in direct opposition with my wishes."

"Yes, sir."

I disconnect and turn to her. "You are a free woman and have a guard at your disposal. He will answer any questions you have and make any arrangements you need for life outside the palace walls whenever and wherever you wish to go."

"I don't understand why you want me to come home with you. Why you want to help me...with babies. I...I know you must have women pushing each other down to be with you. Is this some kind of game? Find the homeliest woman you can and—"

"Be very careful with the words you use to describe my princess," I growl.

"Markellan, this is insane. I'm not the woman you want to be your princess. Surely you must see that. I have no social standing, and I'm horribly awkward and shy. I'm also afraid of almost everything. I'm too much of a coward to join you on this adventure. Or any adventure, really."

"How can you think yourself a coward? You left the only life you knew to go after the life you really want."

She looks down at her lap as if she is ashamed. "But I didn't. I left the only life I knew and made one for myself that is very similar to the one I had, just with fewer wimples."

I pick up her hand, kiss it. "Don't you believe in fate at all? We met twenty years ago by chance in the very same place we found each other today. You have carried my most prized childhood possession with you since that day. I'm usually a man who pays little attention to coincidence, but even I can't deny there is something between us. Can you? Can you really walk away without even looking to see what might happen?"

"I think you are mistaking your very sweet, sincere desire to be my knight in shining armor with fated romance. You probably just feel responsible for me, like you did when we were children. But I'm not the kind of woman who is made for the kind of passion you require—"

I don't let her finish. With a low growl deep in my throat, I fist my hands in her hair and yank her head back, my tongue penetrating deep when she opens her mouth in a surprised gasp.

Chapter Four

Violet

He buries his hands in my hair, kissing me.

Me! Me who's never been kissed by anyone. And these are not starter kisses. Oh no, not at all.

Slow deep kisses, his mouth gliding, slipping and sliding over mine.

I hear my inner-spinster howling in protest, and I ignore her. How many women get their first kiss in a limo with a prince?

He slants his mouth firmly over mine, plundering, nibbling, sucking. Invading. The man doesn't simply kiss—he's making love to my mouth, making it feel all hot and swollen.

I'm going to be outraged. Any minute now.

His hands drop from my hair to my breasts, moving possessively, cupping and plumping them. His thumbs glide over my nipples, making them feel sharp and achy with want.

I don't know what I'm doing, so I grab a fistful of his suit jacket and just hold on. Let him plunder. Let him drag me into this dark passion. I'm drowning in him, in his scent and masculine power. Please, don't anyone throw me a life preserver. Places low in my belly clench. I ache around the emptiness between my legs. My skin is hot, my blood heating it as it boils and rushes swiftly through my veins.

And then he stops, resting his forehead against mine, his breathing shallow and fast. "Tell me again how passionless you are, my little lamb."

I bring my fingertips to my now tender lips. "I don't...how...what did you do to me?"

With gentleness, he pushes a lock of hair off my face. "I think I just woke you up. How do you feel?"

"I don't know. Markellan, this is..."

"Don't tell me it's crazy. You've already said that." He brings my hand back up and kisses it again. "In Kentigen, we have a custom similar to what you would call a honeymoon here, but it happens before the wedding."

I'm not following at all, but he keeps talking.

"The groom has one week to prove himself to the bride. If he can pleasure her enough, take care of all her needs, and show her his capacity to be a husband, she will grant the marriage. Give me a week. In the palace. Let me prove my worth to you. And if at the end of our honeymoon, you choose to return to your country, I will make sure you are well taken care of."

My heart nearly stops when I take in everything he just said, which I admit is taking longer than usual because I'm still befuddled from that kiss. "You want to get married? To *me*?"

"You want to have a baby. I'm offering to put mine inside you. And yes, I would prefer we marry. But if you find me lacking..."

He trails off when I snort.

"You want to get pregnant. You said it was worth leaving the convent for."

"I kind of assumed I would use a sperm bank when I could afford it."

He growls under his breath. I think I hear something about nobody else's sperm gets in my body, but I can't be sure I'm hearing anything right this evening. I'm probably dreaming. Or in a coma.

How sad is it that my life is so much more exciting when I'm comatose?

"So, let me just run this down so when I tell my new therapist, the one I'm going to hire tomorrow, about the crazy dream I had, I get all the details right. After a childhood encounter twenty years ago, you think that running into each other again today means we are somehow destined to be together, despite the fact that you are a prince and I am almost-a-nun and have no worldly experience whatsoever. You want to take me to your palace and get me pregnant, and if after our 'honeymoon'

I want to return home, you'll let me go, even if I'm pregnant with your baby. If I choose to stay, you want to marry me and take me away from my lonely life of solitude and frozen dinners, making me a princess."

He sits back, amused with me for some reason. "First of all, I have no doubts that you will stay and become my princess. I don't think I'll need a full week to convince you. And second, there is no 'if.' I guarantee, I will impregnate you in a week, of that I am also very sure."

"You're very arrogant."

"Perhaps. I intend to fill you with my body so many times and in so many positions you may not walk for days, but you *will* get pregnant."

I swallow. Hard. I don't even think I know what any of that means.

"Have I shocked you?"

"Yes."

"Good. I've just barely begun. I don't want you agreeing to something you don't understand the terms to. So I'll tell you more." Possessive fire burns in his gaze. "I'm very sexually aggressive and dominant to the bone, my little lamb. And that is exactly what you want. What you need."

I gasp, indignation rushing into me, but words don't surface. Things I should say like, no or that's not true, are stuck in my throat. I'm not sure they are true. I don't know what I want or what I need. But I'm convinced Markellan knows. That somehow he sees into my soul and can reach right into it. He's overwhelming, and I want to be overwhelmed.

"I'm a big man, Violet. Everywhere, but I know how to use my body to make you tremble and moan and cry out my name in pleasure. I know how to make you beg for my cock, and when I give it to you, when we're both so needy we'll die if I don't fuck you, I will make you come more times than is advisable. Every inch of my cock was made for your pleasure, and it will touch you in places you only dreamed of. And when you are boneless and sated and nearly unconscious, I will come inside you. I will come long and hard and so deep that when I fill you with my hot seed, I will coat your insides, lamb."

I can't speak. I don't have any words. Nothing that can be said after his words anyway. I don't know if I'm in shock or just waiting to wake up. And he doesn't even look winded after saying all that. I can barely suck in a breath. It's like my lungs have collapsed on no available air. I've never been spoken to like that. With such frank sexuality. I've never even been looked at with sexual interest before and now I'm...what am I?

Shocked? Yes. But more. Intrigued? That isn't a strong enough word. Scared? Oh, yes. That too.

The car stops.

"We're at the airport. My jet is ready. Anything you need, we can acquire in Kentigen. I promise if you choose to return, I will make sure you and the child are taken care of. You needn't worry about losing your job or your apartment. What do you say?"

His glittering gaze challenges me, dares me. Reminds me that he somehow knows the things I've never said aloud, my secret fantasies, the ones hidden deep inside my heart. Desires I didn't think would ever be fulfilled. And here is my chance.

I stare at him in silence, feeling utterly torn. There are a thousand reasons why I absolutely cannot get on that plane with him.

Dare I do something so impulsive? So crazy? So unlike me? On the other hand, dare I go back to my life the way it is? The apartment with not even a plant in it that needs me? A life barren of anything important?

If this were a dream, which it still might be, I might let him take me. Show me the passion I've never experienced. Never dared to want. Be the focus of his unrelenting sensual energy. I rub the coin in my hand. Can I face myself in the mirror if I don't take this Cinderella chance?

"Be brave, Violet. Trust me."

I look into his eyes, so dark, fringed by even darker lashes. There's something else in his eyes. Something I hadn't seen earlier. A vulnerability.

Oh, I'm probably one of the many women in this world who fall for that look. The urge to be needed is strong. The idea that somehow I have something he needs is like a drug.

This is the strangest coma ever.

"All right, I'll go with you."

Chapter Five

Markellan

I asked Tara, Princess Tara, my sister, to keep our arrival low-key. I should have known that was a mistake.

Tara can't resist tormenting me, and as we climb out of the helicopter, I see she has the entire household assembled in some sort of formal reception line. My bride is staring agog at the castle and the line of servants and royal guard all in uniform.

I'll admit it's good to be home. As soon as my feet touch the lawn, something peaceful steals over me. I'm on my turf now—literally. Violet doesn't stand a chance.

I give my sister a dirty look and go right to our mother, kissing each cheek. "My Queen." She raises one brow at me and I know I will have some serious explaining to do.

While I was distracted, Tara made a move on Violet. Damn it. She's ushering her into the house like they are best friends, and Violet looks back at me with wide, nervous eyes. Oh hell. Tara is and always has been, my trouble-making older sister. She thinks she's hilarious when she gets in my business, and I can see she plans to get as much information as she can out of poor Violet.

I catch up to them in the parlor where tea has been set out.

"You must be famished. Here, let me get a plate for you." Tara doesn't let her answer, just goes about stacking sandwiches and cake on the plate as if I maybe hadn't fed the girl on the plane.

Who does she think I am? Of course I looked after Violet. I will *always* look after Violet.

Tara is pouring tea and babbling. "You can't imagine my surprise when my sweet brother asked me to get some clothes and necessities for you. He's never brought a woman home before, so you'll have to excuse me if I get too excited. I always wanted a sister."

"Tara—"

She doesn't even look at me. "Pieter says that the two of you met as children. How romantic." She continues babbling until she wears Violet down, who surprises us all by telling us a story about the monastery.

Good. I'm glad she's coming out of her shell. Though my mother appears to wonder what I've gotten myself into dragging a nun from another country home.

"When I am queen," my sister begins.

Hell. She's been spouting that line since she could talk and it's always something outrageous.

"I don't understand," Violet says, looking at me. "The heir is your sister?"

My mother smiles and puts down her tea. "Our culture is matrilineal. My kingdom reverts to my eldest daughter. Darling, how much did you not explain to Violet about our culture?"

I'm about to speak when Tara gets a dangerous, absolutely giddy look in her eye. "Come, Violet. I shall show you to your room and get you a bath drawn while I tell you absolutely everything you need to know about our country."

"I think I can handle it, Tara."

"Oh, no, brother. I insist. It will be my absolute pleasure to tell her everything."

The only reason I don't stop her is Violet seems drawn to my bubbly sister. I think she needs a female friend, even if it is the brattiest woman in the world. I just hope she doesn't run screaming away when she finds out all I've neglected to tell her about our culture.

Violet

TARA LEFT ME NEARLY twenty minutes ago after talking my ear off while I soaked in the tub made for some kind of giant. At first, I felt so modest in front of her. I've never been naked in front of anyone, but she was flitting around the room and babbling so much that I just quickly got under the bubbles and forgot my embarrassment soon after.

Well, until she told me about the honeymoon. Thankfully, she thought to do so with a few glasses of champagne, which made the whole thing easier to take and yet even more surreal.

Now, I wait for my groom, I guess.

He has his own wing of the palace, a lovely apartment suite filled with a mixture of modern, masculine style and antiquities I'm itching to research. He was right that I would be interested. The friendly boy in the museum was my favorite memory of childhood after my parents' death. Ever since, I've been drawn to old things. Preserving them. Being around them.

If you'd told me I'd be in that boy's apartment twenty years later wearing his silky black robe and drinking champagne, I'd have never believed you.

I finally get brave and open the door I've been avoiding.

His bedroom.

Oh, wow. His sinful, decadent bedroom.

His *lair*.

The masterpiece is the enormous hand-carved bed gracing the center of the room and covered in silks and velvets of black and deep red.

His bed is draped in beaded, lush velvet panels with gold tasseled rope ties as if we're still in medieval times. I imagine it must be like a dark cave of debauchery when they are closed.

This champagne is going to my head. I've only had a few experimental glasses of wine since I've been out on my own. I'm a bit light-headed now, whether from the drink, the hot bath, the travel, the extreme change in circumstance, or just being surrounded by such tangible sensuality, I don't know. But I can guess.

Part of me wants to drink more. Get drunk. Maybe when I wake up, my coma will be gone.

No. I set my glass down on a coaster. I don't want to be drunk. I want to experience everything.

I think. I find the chest in the corner, the one Tara told me was brought in specifically for my honeymoon. I lift the lid slowly, carefully like I'm afraid the contents might bite. They won't. But some may pinch. Some vibrate. Some tickle.

I peer into the wooden box full of items designed to enhance my pleasure. There are lotions in ornate glass bottles, and ornate glass items that are not bottles, but phallic shaped. A feathered stick. Scarves. Restraints. An item that looks suspiciously close to Sister Elena's massager for her muscle stiffness. I close the lid. I don't know how to use anything in it. But Markellan does. Apparently, all men in Kentigen are trained in the use of the honeymoon chest. Most women in the country have their own treasure trove until they get this one, so probably nothing in it is confusing to them. Sexual pleasure is encouraged here.

What can he want with me? I don't even know how to pleasure myself very well. I've managed to get the job done, but I didn't know they made the things in that box to assist. He's going to regret bringing me here.

I close the lid and continue exploring. His scent lingers in the room, an intoxicating mixture of man and unnamed spice and virility

Approaching the ornate mirror on the wall, I trace the intricate work and stare at the woman looking back at me. What does he see in her? She's so plain. Mousy.

"I was afraid you'd have already made arrangements with Con to get the hell out of here after spending time with my sister. Instead, you're in my bedroom wearing my robe. I am very, very pleased." His voice breaks through my pity party.

I meet Markellan's eyes in the mirror and feel the pulse in my neck scrabbling like it's trying to race away.

He's so beautiful. Like a fantasy come to life. A fallen angel in the flesh more like. But beautiful all the same. I don't think he belongs here on earth. He's standing still as a statue, waiting for me to say something.

Anything, Violet.

"You have a lovely home."

Well, that was something. Not a very good something, but something.

He laughs and removes his jacket. "Thank you. How are you feeling?"

"I'm well, thank you." I bite my lip as he unrolls the sleeves of his shirt. "Why are we being so polite?"

"I have no idea."

"Your sister filled me in about some of your country's more unique customs."

We're still holding each other's gazes in the mirror. It seems safer this way.

"The rest of the world finds us a bit of a curiosity, I'll admit. But we seem to do all right."

My skin is heating, but not from a blush for a change. It's remembering his hands on me in the car. The way his tongue felt in my mouth. Goodness, the air in this country must be laced with some kind of decadent pheromone.

He walks toward me, but I don't turn around. Just watch his approach in the mirror.

"So in addition to passing property along the mother's lines here, it seems you revere women more than most of the world."

"Revere is a soft word for it, lamb. The men of my kingdom *worship* women." He's right behind me now. I can feel his hot breath on my neck. "We admire and adore and glorify the female mind, spirit...body." He reaches for my hand and brings the inside of my wrist to his mouth for a soft, wet kiss. "When a boy turns eighteen, he is instructed in the arts of lovemaking so that his future bride will not suffer the sexual advances of a selfish lover, but rather one so attuned to her body that she will blossom under his hands, his mouth, his love." I shiver. "The highest penalized crime in our country is for that of inflicting pain or damage to a woman or child. We take oaths to protect our women with our lives. We're taught to do so from childhood. You're safer here than anywhere else on the planet."

He raises his eyes from my wrist and looks at me, deliberately letting all that he is thinking about doing to me show on his face. I don't think safe is the word I would choose when I see the way he's eyeing me in the mirror. I feel like a snack for a hungry lion. Yet, his country's politics intrigue me.

"It's very different here. You and the guards seem so...I don't know...masculine. Alpha. Is it difficult to worship or revere women, even though we are weaker than you?"

He cocks his head and regards me carefully. "A real man is at his strongest, most virile, when he knows he has pleasured his woman, protected her well, and cared for her every desire. A happy woman, one who is cherished and regarded for her strengths is, in return, a woman who makes her man even stronger. Don't be fooled by the matriarchy; I can assure you the worshiping goes both ways. One sex is not better than the other, my country is just better at promoting a better relationship between the two. You will see. If you stay, of course."

"I'm used to men thinking...I don't know...that they are better, stronger."

"A real man is fearless, courageous, and loyal. He is a protector and does no harm unless it is to protect. I know my power, lamb, but I do not misuse it."

I nod. This really is a dream. I know that now. It's like I handpicked him. Made him up. Hand-wrote the politics of his kingdom in my teenage diary.

"My mother taught me to believe in myself, to know I will succeed if my intentions are clear and my actions align." He fingers the silk robe on my shoulder. "She also taught me to seek a woman who offers tenderness, wisdom, patience, and nurturing. One who is also courageous and loyal. An empowered woman is not fragile. She is strong and righteous and will stand by her lover. Men and women make each other better. There is no need for oppression of either sex."

I swallow hard on the champagne trying to fizz back up my throat. "And the ...lovemaking?"

His nostrils flare and he inhales sharply. "Yes, lamb? What do you want to know about the lovemaking?"

"It seems like it's pretty important here."

"Sex is sacred, Violet. Touching, kissing, intimacy...perfect bliss between lovers is the ideal we strive for."

"What if I'm not good at it? Maybe you won't want me to stay."

"Is that your fear? Look in the mirror," he directs me.

As I do, he wraps an arm around my waist and hugs me to the erection grinding into my backside. My head falls back, exposing my neck and he uses his other hand to trace a delicate path down to my collarbone, then very gently, beneath the panel of the robe. I shiver, melting into the hard wall of man behind me.

He bites my earlobe while I watch as if we are two different people. That can't be me. I've never looked like that before. Ripe and ready. Sexual.

He starts planting kisses up my neck, nibbling as he goes back to my ear, licking it and sucking on the lobe. His eyes are on the mirror as his fingers toy my breast. He pinches a nipple gently, the pert bud getting harder in his hand, while he watches my face in the mirror. My eyes slide closed.

Who am I?

I want to feel his hand and lips on me everywhere, want him inside me.

The hand on my breast stills. I feel him smile next to my ear, and my eyes open. The smile that teases his lips is almost devilish. His hand moves from my breast to my ribs underneath, rubbing firmly. He skims the skin as his magic fingers go lower and then lower still, causing me to shudder.

I feel him behind me. Hard. So hard. And big. I should worry about that, but his hand goes lower yet, delving into the place I've only just begun to know myself since leaving the convent. I ache for him there. I may only have vague ideas about how the mechanics of sex go, but my body seems to be catching on.

"So wet," he whispers in my ear, and I convulse when his finger glides through my folds.

I can feel him pushing his fingers, strumming on the pearl he finds there. The robe falls open and I see his hand cupping me, his fingers moving, my breasts heaving. It's too much. Shudders rack my body and I start to slip, would fall to the ground if Markellan wasn't holding me to him.

I look down at my feet. "Don't... don't look at me, please," I beg, quivering. I am engulfed by the sensations he is causing.

"Why not?" he asks.

"I don't ... I don't know. It's indecent." I whisper, still not able to look at him.

"You are beautiful. Why do you want to hide it?" he asks with concern in his voice.

He thinks I'm beautiful.

"It's just so..." I stammer, unable to complete my thoughts. This is all so new.

"Naughty?"

"Yes," I admit.

"That's the whole point, lamb. I want you to be naughty. I want you to be naughty for me," he says.

"Oh, God."

"Good girl," he says hoarsely, pressing harder on my swollen clit, making my moans turn to cries. "Look into the mirror," he commands again.

I look up. My hair is disheveled, my eyes glassy, my lips plump.

"I want you to stay," he says simply, bringing me back to the conversation we were having before he touched me.

He wants me to stay. Here. In Kentigen.

I begin to feel a bit of that empowerment he spoke of earlier. I may be the one who had an orgasm, but he looks just as on edge.

He gently ties the robe together again. "I'm going to take a shower. Shall I send for a tray for you or did you have enough refreshments downstairs?"

"I'm fine." I couldn't eat right now if I tried. My stomach is too jittery. My legs too shaky. My mind too busy. My body too needy.

"Usually, a honeymooning couple will retire to an isolated location for their week of intimacy. I had an idea that you might feel more comfortable here where you know civilization is not too far away. The staff has stocked the kitchen well but have been instructed to leave us alone unless we ask for them. There are intercoms in every room, and as you are aware, Con is your personal attendant. When he is off duty, you will still be protected. At any time you wish, they are available to you by pushing an intercom. Otherwise, we are alone."

I suck in a breath. He's making sure I feel safe. That I don't feel trapped. I'm sure that must come at some cost to him, yet he puts my needs ahead of his own.

And he leaves me standing in his bedroom. Knowing he's naked under the spray of the shower. Knowing soon he'll be naked in front of me.

Chapter Six

Markellan

When I come out of the shower, my bride is drunk.

I wasn't gone that long, I swear.

Damn it.

She's sitting in the middle of my bed, wearing my robe, and drinking champagne straight from the bottle.

"Look at you," she says unsteadily. "It's like someone poured velvet over steel to sculpt your body. You have no flaws. And we're going to make a baby. But seriously, you're absolutely rippling with muscle. Like I can see them rippling right now. Maybe you should stand still."

"I am standing still, love."

She hiccups. "Did you know that your shoulders are like huge? And they taper down so nicely into your waist. Like this—" She makes some vague hand movement to show me how my body tapers. "Also your hair."

"My hair?"

"Yeah. Not on your head. On your navel. I didn't even know you had hair there, but look at it. It's like a dark, silky trail that disappears beneath your towel. You're naked under that towel, aren't you?"

I am not a strong enough man for this. She's a lush fantasy come to life *in my bed*, and I can't take her. Not tonight. Not while she's drunk.

Fuck.

"How about a pot of coffee?" I ask.

"No. But you know what? I have to pee!" She starts scrabbling, sliding on my slippery bed coverings and flashing me bits of lush, pale skin, and my entire body tightens.

Mine.

Instead of doing what I want, I help her down so she doesn't break her neck. While she's in the bathroom, I put on pajama bottoms, willing my cock to rest. When she comes back out, she throws the robe onto the floor. "All right. I'm ready."

Fuck me.

How am I supposed to not fuck her? She's naked, her luscious curves inviting me to take handfuls. Just take. I'm on the razor's edge of raw need—my hunger has never felt so dark and...depraved. I want to drag her into it with me. And there she is. Willing and naked. Her inhibitions stifled by alcohol. No one would blame me if I took her now. She just asked me to.

But the first time I am inside her body, she will remember me, damn it. She will beg for me. She will need me.

It won't be like this.

I try to help her onto the bed, ignoring all the supple skin and places inviting me to taste. She flops down onto her stomach in the middle of the bed facing sideways.

"Lamb, let's get you under the covers." Fierce possessiveness consumes me. What I want to do is stretch flat on top of her. Skin to skin, pinning her to the bed, letting her feel the full weight of my body. I'd nudge her thighs apart, tease her with my cock. Is she still wet from coming on my fingers in front of the mirror?

I want to turn all my years of training and mastery of lovemaking to taming her lush curves, nibbling the backs of her knees, the insides of her thighs. I want to bathe every inch of her body with my tongue. I'd stretch her hands above her head and drag my tongue down her spine. Slowly, so fucking slowly. I want to feel her shake and tremble beneath me, moan for me to enter her sweet pussy. I want...hell, she's snoring.

Violet

ONE THING I CAN SAY about Kentigen that is not in its favor is that it's very bright. Painfully bright. I think about pulling the blanket over my head, but it hurts too much to move. I am sure my head is going to fall right off.

"Lamb, drink this," I hear a disembodied voice say. That's when I remember how very un-disembodied he was last night. He was very, very embodied. That's when I remember what I said to him. And oh my goodness. The mirror. And...

"You want this, I promise."

I blink, close my eyes, and blink them again. I'm completely naked under the blankets, and I don't remember much after using the bathroom.

"I see all your questions flashing across your face and I will answer them all. Drink this; it's my sister's famous hangover cure and it tastes awful but works. Yes, you are naked. Yes, you are still a virgin. Yes, you did say some curious things about what was under my towel. And no, you didn't dream coming on my hand. That happened before you drank too much."

I sip the awful smelling potion in the glass. "I'm sorry." Ugh, this stuff is awful.

"What are you sorry for?"

"Getting drunk. Acting foolish." Ruining our first night.

"I enjoyed watching you be foolish. Let me take care of you this morning."

And he does. He forces me to drink the vile cure, but it really does work. He runs me yet another bath. Feeds me a breakfast he cooks himself. And when I'm feeling more myself, his eyes nearly change color when he glowers at me suddenly and says, "I want to make you come on my tongue."

I nearly spit out the water I just sipped. My skin blazes. My mind races. "Wh-what?"

Gone is the nearly civilized gentleman he's been all morning. The one who turned his head while I got out of bed naked because I felt modest. The one who made a smiley face on my pancake with whipped cream. *This* man is an untamed barbarian. His whole body is coiled and ready to pounce on me like a panther.

He's been wearing just his pajama bottoms all morning, and I thought I was accustomed to his bare chest, but when he stands, I find I'm once again drunk—just not on champagne this time.

Him. I'm drunk on him.

He's huge, looming over me as he offers me his hand as if we were in a fancy restaurant and he didn't just offer to use his tongue on me. I stare up at him, my eyes roving over his thick chest, those rippling abs, and that trail...that soft trail I follow with my eyes into his waistband where a very not-soft erection pushes against his pants.

For me? We weren't even talking about sex. He must have just been sitting across from me thinking about it and ...I made him this hard.

Me? Really?

I don't know how to think. What to feel. The only way I'm used to feeling is a little uptight and a lot prissy. "It's...morning. It's not appropriate to have relations right now."

He chuckles. When he speaks it is with a new firmness—a deep, quiet, commanding voice. All confidence. "Appropriate? Nothing I intend to do to you over the next seven days is appropriate, Violet. I'm going to fill you with come, over and over. I'm going to learn every inch of your body, what pleases you and what makes you shiver. If something frightens you a little, I'll push even harder, making you face every dark and depraved fantasy we have."

"You shouldn't speak to me this way."

"I think you like the way I speak to you. And I know you like the way I made you come last night." His hand is still outstretched. "I can't wait to taste you again."

"Again?"

"I licked your sweetness off my fingers last night. Every last drop. Have you ever tasted yourself, Vi?"

I shake my head quickly. I feel ashamed but I don't know if it's because I'm embarrassed by his words or by the fact that it never occurred to me to taste myself.

It's such a raw thing to hear. To imagine.

"You're sweet. And tangy. And if you're a very good girl, I'll let you taste yourself from my cock after I use it to make you come over and over again."

The words are like a swift punch of primal intensity. I never thought I would do such things. That anyone would want me to do something so wicked. "You're the devil."

"I'm your devil. There is no shame in anything we do together."

"I don't know if I can believe that." It feels like my whole life has been spent hiding from the kinds of things he is making me want. "I feel like I'm being broken into pieces."

"Passion is going to break us both into pieces. It's supposed to. It will shatter us and then put us back together again, stronger than before. You'll see," his voice rasps, sounding even thicker and deeper, the sound inflaming the growing warmth that had begun building inside me.

But I don't know what to do with the warmth inside me. The growing awareness of not just the prince, but myself. "Why don't you want someone who already knows this? Wouldn't it be better? For you? Don't you want someone who has experience?"

"You misunderstand. I've never experienced these feelings before either. The honeymoon is sacred here. I have training, yes. But I don't give my seed indiscriminately. You are special. This between us is special. Take my hand. Let me show you."

An acceptance starts happening inside me. Something that feels hopeful for the first time in my adult life. Maybe fairy tales don't really come true, but this man has gone through an awful lot of trouble to make me believe they do. There's no reason I can think of that he would do this all for me unless I truly am what he wants.

I let him help me up, and he pulls me right into his massive body, cushioning his hard, throbbing erection into my soft body. I do something that surprises us both when my arms loop around his neck. He gifts me with a slow, arrogant smile before he crushes his lips against mine.

He isn't just kissing me. He's claiming me. He takes my mouth, licking and nipping. He slants my mouth and deepens the kiss, slow and long, and I ache deep where he touched me last night. He groans a savagely masculine sound and his kisses change. Urgent. Punishing. Hard.

And I love it.

He rips away from me, the look in his eyes promising dark pleasures and an edge of danger. "Do you wish to leave? Now might be your last chance. If you stay, you will come to my bed now and not leave it until my seed is planted deep inside you. Several times. Do you understand?"

I nod.

His nostrils flare. "You're wet, aren't you?"

"Yes," I whisper.

"My kisses make you that way, Violet, because you are mine." He uses my hand to cup his erection. "And this is what your kisses do to me. Because I am yours."

I gasp in shock, but my hand cups him harder. He's throbbing there, pulsing. For me.

The fat, mushroom head pokes out from the top of the waistband. The tip is kissed in wetness, and I don't think, I just run my fingertip in the dew. He hisses as I swirl it around. He pulls me tighter to him, grinding into me. "You're going to make me forget all my training if you keep touching me. I won't be able to stop myself."

I raise my eyes to his and cover the head of his erection in my hand. "Are you going to ravage me, Your Majesty?"

Heat flares in his eyes at my bratty tone. "That's what you want, isn't it? My sweet, pure Violet wants me to fuck her like a feral beast, doesn't she?"

Hungers from deep inside me pull to the surface, drowning me in desire for things I can't even name. But he can. He can take this ache away. He knows what I need, and I can make him give it to me. I let the prudish tone seep into my next words, hoping to fire him up. To make him take me. "Markellan, how do I know what I want? I'm completely innocent, remember? You're going to have to show me *everything.*"

He growls and drags me to the floor, pulls open my robe, and bares me to him. He pins my hands to the floor near my head and growls into my mouth while kissing me, taking my own moans into his. His erection is leaving a trail of wetness on my stomach as he pushes into me. Out of instinct, my legs wrap around him and my hips thrust up.

"Do you need to come again, Violet? Is your little wet pussy greedy for me to make it come again?"

"Yes," I say, urging him to drive into me instead of holding himself above me the way he is.

"Tell me your pussy is wet for me."

I bite my lip and stare up at him. "I don't think I can say that. I'm too..."

"Do not tell me you are too shy. Not now when I can smell your desire. Tell me how wet your pussy is. Tell me," he demands.

"My pussy...I'm so wet for you, Markellan. I want you so badly. My pussy is wet. So wet."

"Good girl."

With that, he moves down my body and before I can protest his absence, he pushes my legs wide open and stares at me. At my pussy. I said the word, now I can think it.

He's staring at my pussy with a fierce expression on his face. One that is brutally masculine. He makes me wait, exposed and vulnerable, while he stares. "You are fucking perfect. I'm going to fuck you with my mouth. I'm going to taste how much you want me."

My hips jolt at the first touch of his tongue. In the back of my mind, the inner prude is putting up a fuss. This is wrong. Wrong to let him use his mouth on me there. Wrong to be with a man not my husband. Wrong to enjoy the silky slide of his tongue like a wanton whore. But when he groans his pleasure and the sound vibrates on my ...on my *clit*, I ignore the prude. I am allowed pleasure, and this is pleasure like nothing I've ever felt.

He drags his tongue up and down, slurping as he does, the sound of it so lewd. So filthy. His hands slide under my bottom, pulling me into his mouth. I think I might be dying. It's too much. And then he pushes his tongue inside my channel.

He's literally fucking me with his tongue. I become a wild thing, bucking and trembling under his face, and he has to squeeze my ass to keep me in place for his relentless tongue.

I twist to move away. It's too much, but he holds me harder.

"I can't."

"You will." He licks me from the bottom of my slit to the top, curling his tongue. "You will. You are mine. Mine to eat and mine to fuck."

My blood roars in my head, and I can't get a deep enough breath. I thought last night in front of the mirror was intense, but that was nothing compared to this. There is no mercy here. He intends to use my body to unlock things I had no intention of giving him. There is terrible danger in pleasure. And terrible pleasure in danger.

My body clenches in need. Release from the torture dangles in front of me, but only if I jump headlong off the cliff into the abyss. Markellan reaches up and palms my breast, pinching the nipple, and I leap over the edge, screaming as the pleasure explodes in sonic waves.

Breath is sawing in and out of my lungs when he rises above me, his dark eyes searing me, a wicked grin curling his glossy, wet lips, his voice, strong and commanding demands, "Again."

Chapter Seven

Markellan

I can't get enough of this woman. The sweet, mouth-watering taste I had of her pussy only makes me want more. She was so responsive to me, coming so hard and flooding my mouth with her intoxicating juices, I have to have more.

I make my way back down to where I need to be, sucking on her skin as I go.

She is languid with desire, spreading her thighs for me, welcoming my mouth. Her back arches, ready for me to taste her again. I part her swollen lips and lick as if I were starving. As if I hadn't just made her come. Her body melts into me as my tongue pushes deeper into her slit, wetness flooding between her thighs and down my chin.

Again she arches her back, pulling my tongue in deeper. I become a man possessed, eating her sweet cunt, lapping at her feverishly. Her body begins to shake. "That's it, angel. Come on my face again."

"Oh...that sounds so dirty. So filthy...so oh, so good."

I smile into her pussy. She's the perfect partner for me. Making her *want* to be depraved is my goal. And I am succeeding. "Such a dirty girl. You fooled everyone, didn't you? They all think you're a good girl, but I knew. I knew right away what this little pussy needed, didn't I?"

She screams in pleasure when I take her clit inside my mouth, sucking and tugging, as another orgasm rolls through her. She thrashes beneath me, and I do know what she needs.

My cock. Pumping inside her.

God knows I need it too.

All that training, and I'm going to take my princess on the floor next to our breakfast table? Conceive my first child on the carpet? When there is a perfectly good, large bed in the other room, too.

I steel my reserve. No. Not like this.

I roll off her, my breath heaving. I need a moment to compose myself. "Go, get in my bed," I demand, used to getting my way and knowing she needs me to be in control in order for her to submit to her own desires. To my desires. Some women need to be in control, and some, like Violet, need to be in submission in order to fully engage in passion.

"Hmm?" she says fuzzily, as if her brain is not connecting all the way. Good.

"Now, Violet. Go get in my bed before I take you like an animal on the floor."

She scampers up and into the other room while I collect myself, breathing through the pain of my desire.

And then I follow.

She's sitting on the bed, watching me warily. I take my time, lighting all the candles, letting her anticipation build. I pull the honeymoon chest out and open it slowly, watching all the thoughts flit across her face in succession.

I don't put any music on. I want to hear every rasp of her breath, gasps, and moans.

I kneel in front of her, wanting her to feel my reverence. "Your body is my playground now. I am going to do whatever I want to you. Do you trust me?"

"Yes," she whispers.

"Good girl."

"Take off the robe and lie down."

Her breath hitches, but she shimmies out of the robe and does what I say. I pull out the scarves and her eyes go round. "This will enhance your pleasure, lamb."

I decide against restraining her legs this time. I want to feel them wrapped around me later.

I pour some massage oil onto her skin. It's a very special blend, and as the aroma fills the air, she moans before I even touch her. "My people have spent centuries perfecting this fragrance, love. Can you feel the scent working already? The air you breathe is an aphrodisiac. The oil of a very special flower found only here in Kentigen. The scent will help relax you. My hands will do the rest."

I begin to rub the sweet-smelling oil into her breasts, massaging them firmly. God, I love her tits. "So gorgeous, so responsive," I murmur before my mouth descends on one taut peak, my warm, wet tongue moving in deliberate circles as my hands continue sliding down her skin. My slick hands glide over her hips and stomach. I force myself off her breast and massage up and down her legs until she is languid and relaxed.

"Close your eyes."

She does so with no hesitation, and my need for her clutches me like a vice.

Not yet.

I pull another vial out of the basket and drip some of the liquid onto the tip of a toy, then a few drops onto her wet folds. She twitches against the restraints as the lubricant tingles icily along her sensitive lips. "That feels cold, doesn't it, love? We call this oil 'frosty kiss.' Keep your eyes closed." I push the button on the toy and a soft buzz fills the room. Her skin blooms with goose bumps and then her body convulses when I touch the toy to her pussy. "Open your legs." I use the small tip of the toy to explore her, watching her face as pleasure dances across it almost uncomfortably. I push it inside her, causing her to yank and pull at the restraints, as she cries out and her eyes fly open.

Then I find it. The single point inside her. Her eyes roll back as the vibrations shoot through her in waves. Her back arches and the bedposts creak in resistance. A series of feral moans fly out between gasps of air. "You're perfect, Violet."

She only moans in response. My cock is so hard I could drive an iron spike into the ground with it, but watching her come is addicting. I bring out the feather as she comes down from her orgasm, tickling her lightly as her body continues to spasm. I slowly bring her down, down, down. Back to earth. Her eyes are glassy and she's so goddamned beautiful I have to put a hand over my heart to keep it from beating right out of my chest.

"That was..." she says, dazed.

"It certainly was. Are you ready for me?"

She nods, but as I slide my pants all the way off, my large, angry, ready-to-do-some-damage cock springs out, and her eyes round with shock and maybe a little horror.

That little bit of fear is intoxicating. "You're going to like this, Vi. You'll come to take my cock whenever and wherever I tell you. Surrendering to me will be the easiest thing you ever do." I ease back up her body, letting my dick settle on her stomach between us, my balls nestled against that soft pussy, and kiss her until she relaxes again.

"Spread your legs more, angel." I rub the thick slippery head of my dick up and down between her lips. When she gets slicker, I push the fat tip of it against her opening. Slowly, I ease inside her. Just the tip, but it feels so amazing.

Her eyes roll up in her head as she pants. I fight every barbarian instinct I have to shove all the way inside. I need to fuck her like I need to breathe.

I grit my teeth, dying to move. She's breathing slower, I can feel her adjusting to my size. She's so tight. Too tight.

I need to go back down on her. She's too tense.

I start to pull back but I'm stopped by Violet's hard thrust up into me. She gasps as I bottom out inside her. I hold very still as she breathes through the shock.

"Sweetheart?"

"I just wanted you so much," she explains. "I needed to feel you inside me all the way."

Well, I'm inside her all the way now, for damn sure. Poor angel just took her own virginity using my cock. That's actually fucking hot. I untie her wrists, needing to know she can hold me if she needs to.

I feel her all around me. Her flesh is pulsing, stretching around my shaft. "You feel better than anything I have ever felt in my life," I tell her, kissing her again. "Your hot pussy is gripping my cock so tightly." Wet, hot silk. "How do you feel?"

Slowly, I start grinding and rocking into her, and she moans.

"Stretched. Full." I pull halfway out and thrust back in. "Oh!"

"Are you mine, Violet?" I ask, knowing the answer from the glazed look in her eyes.

"Yes."

I thrust again, a little harder this time. "Is this my pussy, Violet?"

"Oh, yes. Yes. All yours."

"That's right. You're taking every inch of me now." There's a bit of the cooling lotion left inside her, and it mixes with her hot, wet heat. The sensation is incredible, and I don't know how much longer I can hold out. "Be a good girl and make that pussy come all over my cock."

"I don't think I can come again—" She cries out when I move my hips in a figure eight and grind my pelvis into her clit.

"Yes, you can. I won't come in this pussy until you give me another one. You want my cum, don't you? You want me to fill you up and give you a baby?"

Oh that did it. She's gasping, gripping my biceps. "Yes."

"I want to empty myself into you. That's what you want, isn't it? All my cum, all for Violet. Filling you up. Mating you. *Breeding* you. All you have to do is come one more time, love. Squeeze that pussy around my cock. Drain me."

Violet bucks, arching her back. Close, so close.

"Violet, I've never come inside a woman before. I've never felt another person this way. Just like this. Bare and raw. I want to give you my baby. I want to fuck my baby right into you, right now."

Her pussy floods with lubrication and then starts contracting around me. Squeezing me. Milking me. Her orgasm pushes me over the edge, and my dick starts pistoning in her hard. I've never felt this way before, so untamed and animalistic. I drive into her deep and roar as my hot cum releases inside her. Filling her up just like I promised. My seed is leaking out of her, and I keep thrusting, coming longer and harder than I even thought possible.

I nearly collapse on top of her but don't pull out. "Do you feel all my cum inside you, angel?" My hips weld to her and I keep grinding her into the mattress, forcing all that semen into her channel. "I need you to come again, draw it all up inside you."

"I can't."

My fingers reach between us, and I slide through her slick skin, stroking her clit until her inner walls clench around me again. My body jerks as if I'm coming again too. Aftershocks. I won't move off her until I slip out, and the way I'm feeling right now, I might get hard again first.

We are drenched and sated and probably pregnant. And the week has just begun.

Chapter Eight

Violet

Soaking in the large tub for the third time since we arrived yesterday is a very different experience when sharing it with a prince.

Now I know why the tub is so big.

I'm sitting in front of him, my back to his chest, his legs on either side of me. There are candles on every flat surface of the room and we're drinking water from champagne flutes since I have no interest in another hangover. It's perfect. I really do have the best comas ever. I don't ever want to wake up.

Markellan kisses my neck. "What are you thinking?"

"That I never want to wake up from this dream," I answer truthfully.

He tugs my earlobe with his teeth. "This is real."

"It can't be. It's too perfect. *You're* too perfect."

"I promise you I'm not perfect. You already know I'm arrogant as hell."

"You seem perfect to me."

"That's because I've been giving you blinding orgasms that keep you from looking at my faults too closely."

Well, that is certainly true. I'm not a virgin anymore. I spent most of my life thinking I would always be a virgin. Like Mary. Even when I walked away from the convent, I thought I would remain chaste.

I knew when I left the convent it was the right decision because I didn't have the calling. I never had the calling. I had a fear of what life might be like outside the walls of the convent, so I stayed. And that isn't the right reason to dedicate yourself to a religious vocation.

So, leaving was the right thing. But is living this way the right thing?

How does sex outside of marriage figure in if the honeymoon comes before the wedding? Is it wrong? I keep waiting to feel wrong, to feel guilt and shame. I feel very wicked, but I have no shame about it. I actually like it.

"Are you sore, lamb?"

"Would you think badly of me if I said deliciously sore? I ache everywhere, but it's almost pleasant. Is that normal?"

"God, I hope so."

I hold up my hand and inspect my pruning fingers. "I suppose we should get out. I just..."

His arm squeezes me tightly to him. "You just what? You can tell me anything."

The tenderness I feel from him is overwhelming. I keep finding different facets of him with each passing hour. Who would think a giant his size, used to getting whatever he wants, the same man who dominated me so completely, is also so capable of holding me so sweetly. I'm cherished and protected, yet I know in the passing of a minute, he could resume his barbarian persona, pillaging my body and ravishing my soul. And he wants me to tell him how I feel. How would I put this feeling into words? "I've never felt like this. Like I do right now. Safe and content and in the moment. I'm afraid when we get out of this bath, I'll revert back to the old Violet. The scared one. And she'll be embarrassed about everything we've done and I'll pull away. I want to feel like this forever."

"You've been scared a long time. It would be strange if you changed overnight. My dick is magic, but even I have my limits."

I giggle. "It is magic."

"We might have a few steps backward now and then. This is all new to both of us. It's okay if you get scared and try to pull away a little. I believe you will always come back to me. And I will always wait for you."

"See? You really are perfect."

We get out of the tub and he dries me off gently, so I turn around and return the favor. It's no hardship, exploring his body with a towel. Getting to know where his skin is smooth and where it's covered in dark fur. Where he is marked by scars. Where his muscles are defined, how they flex when I touch them. I drop the towel and rub my hands over his chest. I feel his nipples stiffen when my thumb grazes them. Interesting. My hands slide down to his ab muscles. So tight. I think he's holding his breath as I run my finger down the trench of the center of his six...eight-pack. I circle around him slowly, trailing my hand across his skin, feeling his heat. He's a tower of muscle and his back a wall of pure masculinity. I pause as my hand goes lower. Not sure if I should...

"Do whatever you like, lamb. My body is yours."

I squeeze his...ass. It's so freeing to think the words I've spent my life pushing away. Ass. Pussy. Cock. Clit. His ass is amazing. Round and firm. I keep making my slow circle until I am back to standing in front of him. His body turns me on so much. I have urges that I don't understand. Instincts that are calling me, telling me I'll understand them more if I just allow myself to let the spell take over. So I do. I slide to my knees and look up at him towering over me, his glistening, golden-tanned skin poured over beefy muscle, his thick, black hair slicked back from his face, the severe expression in his eyes so dominant and masculine.

I feel utterly feminine and divine down here. Submissive yet empowered. And I want to know him better. Intimately. I want to take pleasure from pleasing him.

My hands trace up his legs, his perfect calves, his rock-hard thighs. His body is so different from mine. So solid and dense. A fleeting worry of my own soft form invades my brain. Wondering how this perfect specimen of virility could ever be content with my fluffy, round body. But the way he looks at me steals my breath. He could have any woman he wants. He could have more than one at a time, I'm sure. But it's me he's locked his gaze on. Me who has his powerful body tense and ready. I command his attention now.

His cock, red and hard, bobs in front of my face as if he read my thoughts. It's a beast in its own right. Turgid, veined, powerful. I quiet my fears, remembering the pleasure, remembering the man who held me in the bath. I take a deep breath and lick my lips.

"You don't have to—"

"I want to," I say. And I do. Oh, I really do. I want to feel bold.

"Take what you want. It's yours." His deep voice is filled with so much desire that I feel a twinge in my pussy from his words.

My pulse hammers in my ears as I reach to touch him. His cock jerks against my hand, and he hisses in a breath, so I stroke—my hand not fully getting around his girth. I can't believe I actually fit the whole thing inside me. I like its smooth silky texture and the way it pulses against my palms with a throbbing warmth. He is seeping cream from the crown again, but instead of running my finger through the wetness, this time I touch it with the tip of my tongue, tasting my prince for the first time.

He groans and trembles above me, so I do it again, letting his full flavor settle in my mouth, waking up my senses. I don't know what I expected, but I didn't know it would trigger a craving so intense. More. I want more. I put my whole mouth around the head, feeling the weight of him on my tongue, tasting him more fully. I look up at him and he is staring at me with such dark carnality, I pause. And then I suck on the tip hungrily, keeping my eyes on his, feeling my pussy get wet enough to trickle down my thigh. Markellan's hand cups the back of my head possessively, but he just holds it there, letting my mouth widen around him, pulling his cock deeper into my mouth. It feels heavy, powerful. I experiment with bobbing my head to get more in, and swirling my tongue, learning the texture of him, using my hand to cover what my mouth can't. The velvet silk of his skin tastes earthy. He grounds me to the here and now. My body feels so much more mine when he's inside it.

"Your mouth is so fucking hot, Violet. My sweet, innocent Violet, sucking me so damn good," he says, his cock flexing in my mouth. "I love how you're looking at me right now. So pretty with my cock in your mouth, your sweet lips moving over me." I moan at his dirty words, and the vibration makes him close his eyes for a moment. He gathers some composure and stills my head. "You're going to make me come. Is that what you want? Do you want me to fill up your mouth, Violet? I can't give you a baby that way. You'll have to get me hard again to fuck your pussy if you let me come in your mouth."

His sinful promise drives me to resume sucking harder, taking as much of him as I can, trying to get more and more. He groans, his hips pumping against my mouth. I can feel his cock swelling, can feel him losing control as animal urges take over us. Me on my knees on the bathroom floor. Him towering over me like a sex god being worshiped, his dark eyes fierce and commanding.

"Are you sure?" he asks, so I grip his ass in my other hand and squeeze. "I'm going to fill up that hot, little mouth. I'm going to—"

Hot, sticky flavor erupts in my mouth as he roars, pumping and splashing the liquid lava on the roof of my mouth and my tongue. I attempt to drink it all, but swallowing around his cock is difficult. And there is so much of it. I'm trying to keep up, but I feel it leaking from the corners of my mouth as he throbs. He cries out my name, hoarse and satisfied, and when he pulls out, he drops to his knees on the floor with me, pulling me into his barrel-chest. "I think you just drained the life out of me, lamb." His hand slides down, cupping my mound, one finger delving into my sopping wet pussy. "Oh, you are a naughty girl. So wet. You loved sucking my cock, didn't you? Do you love my cum, too? My naughty girl."

I whimper with need, but he knows how to help me, massaging my clit hard until I break in his arms, soaring on a high like I've never felt.

I feel his seed drying on my chest where it dripped down from my mouth. I'm messy and sticky and so, so happy.

"Markellan?"

"Yes, lamb?"

"I think I need another bath already."

Chapter Nine

Markellan

We are on day five of our honeymoon, and I have lost track of the times my Violet has drained me with her sweet mouth and pussy. We're both chafed and exhausted, but I can't get enough of her. I wake up in the middle of the night hard and reaching for her. We've barely been outside. We barely leave my bed.

She's changing, becoming less inhibited with every hour. Her eyes don't lower to the floor or her lap as often as they did when we first met. She doesn't immediately cover herself when the blanket rides down and exposes her breasts like she did at first. Her blushes are less frequent, and she no longer stops herself from touching me or touching herself when the instinct arises.

God, when she touches herself I lose control.

"Are you sleeping, Your Majesty?" she asks, as she continues stroking my hair.

"Nearly." I'm relaxed and replete, my cheek resting on her stomach where our child might be growing already. I never knew this kind of peace before she came to Kentigen, but it only lasts until the next urgency to fuck her comes along and possesses me.

Not a bad way to live. Not bad at all.

My cellphone rings—the first time in days. I reach over her to look. Damn it. I answer gruffly. "Tara, if this isn't an emergency..."

"I'm sorry. I know you're not to be disturbed, but you really have to come to the ball tonight. I've tried to get you out of it several times, but I can't."

Tara is an expert at getting out of things. If she can't do it, I'm fucked. "I'm on my *honeymoon.*"

"I know. I know. Just make a quick appearance and you can leave again. The queen is on a bender."

Fuck. I disconnect the call and blow out all the air in my lungs unhappily. "We have to attend the ball tonight. My mother is insisting." And the queen gets what the queen wants.

Violet stiffens beneath me. "I can't go to a ball. All I have to wear is your bathrobe."

"We'll get you a gown." I sit up and find myself unable to tear my eyes away from her strawberry-topped breasts. They are amazing. White, round fleshy orbs topped like a sundae with rosy nipples that beg me to suck them. So I lean over and take one in my mouth, circling the budded nipple with my tongue. Fuck the ball. I'm staying right here.

"I can't go to a royal ball."

"It won't be that bad, I promise," I say between breasts.

I feel a chill and realize it's Violet. Pulling back from me. Freezing me out.

I rise up on my elbows. "You've already met the queen and the future queen. They are the most imposing ones there and you did fine. Everyone will love you."

She rolls away and slips on the robe. "I won't go. I can't go."

"Why not?"

"I'm a nun."

"I can assure you that you are not a nun. My come is leaking down your leg right now." I hoped that would anger her, force her to hiss like a cat and get us to the bottom of this...whatever it is that's causing her to withdraw. Instead, she gives me a cold look. One that hits me like bricks. I already know her enough to see what she is really saying. "You don't want to come to the ball because you don't think you are going to stay. You think you're going back to America after this."

She shrugs but her eyes are so vacant and cold it feels like she's not even in her body. Like someone else controls her limbs and my Violet is locked away someplace in a tower. "I haven't made any decisions yet, but you have to admit it seems like the most likely outcome."

"Does it?"

"Markellan, we both know I don't fit in your world. What would I do at a ball?"

"Eat, drink, dance. What does anyone do at a ball?"

"I have no idea! I thought they were things that only happened in fairy tales. I didn't realize that there were people who still had them. I don't know how to dance. I don't know how to walk in high heels. I don't even know how to curtsy."

I pull open a drawer and yank out a pair of jeans, stuffing my legs into them without putting on underwear. I just can't be naked when she breaks me. I know it's coming. I can feel the ice crystallizing everything in this room. Including her heart.

How the hell did I allow myself to fall so fast? How did I get so weak? I didn't even try to guard my heart. I'm such an arrogant bastard it never occurred to me I might lose it. "So you learn how to curtsy, wear flat shoes, and just let me hold you on the dance floor." But even I know that the ball isn't what the problem is.

The first sign of real life intrudes on us and she retreats. She hasn't even seen the kingdom yet. The beautiful city lights. The small villages where she'd feel more at home. I want to give her the mountains and freshwater streams. Show her the vineyards that frosts our grapes for the ice wine Kentigen is famous for producing. If I don't find a way to convince her to stay, she'll go back to her country with my babe in her belly just like I told her she could do.

But nothing will be accomplished by forcing her to the ball tonight.

I need air. I need to think. To plan.

To find a way to erase that vacant look in her eyes.

"I will attend the ball without you tonight. But this conversation isn't over." There are two men inside me right now. One is primal and cave-dwelling, demanding that I take my woman now, fuck her into submission. The other is the man I was raised to be. The one who already worships her as my patron goddess. That demands I protect her right to make her own choices.

Fuck that dude. Right now I hate him.

The gym. I need to hit the gym and the bag. Hit it hard. I will pummel the punching bag, attend the ball, and when I return, use my dick to convince her to stay.

When I am leaving I hear her on the comm line. Asking for Con.

She's calling Con. Just like I told her to do if she wanted to leave.

I would give her everything, all of me. My insatiable desire, my need, my determination to cater to her every carnal wish.

If only she'd have me.

Chapter Ten

Violet

My heart is in my throat and I feel sick. "Are you absolutely sure about this?" Tara asks me. "You don't have to do this tonight. There's no rush."

I squeeze her hand. "Thank you for being so kind to me. I've had lots of women friends over the years, but none that would have been able to help with this kind of problem."

I keep thinking about the way Markellan looked this morning. The way I hurt him. The way I wanted him while he stood there in unbuttoned jeans and bare feet. My erotic awareness of him did not dim even then, when I could see I was hurting him.

But it's better this way.

I take a deep breath. It's time. Time to say goodbye.

To the old Violet.

"Miss Violet Havisham," the man announces and all eyes turn to me. It's a new name to them. Tara said it's a small enough kingdom that new would be noticed.

But it's only one set of eyes I'm looking for.

As I descend the grand staircase slowly, and in flats, I see a man weaving through the crowd, his frame large and commanding, until at last he is in front.

Markellan.

Okay, so I know the "nothing but unbuttoned well-worn jeans" look made my insides melt, but I can't say that the outfit he's got on now doesn't do the same thing. Some kind of uniform with all the bells and whistles. Gold braiding and trim accentuate how fine the coat is made, but it is the beast wearing it that stuns me.

And that blatant look of lust in his eyes.

He's looking at me like I'm the most desirable woman in the world, and I can feel his gaze like a caress on every erogenous zone on my body. And some zones I don't think that are meant to be erogenous but suddenly are. My heart is hammering, and my head is telling me to watch my step, I still have about two dozen to get down without tripping on this gown.

He seems to be stalking me with every step closer to the stairs. No hesitation now. There is a power rolling off him. I continue my way down, but he begins going up—two stairs at a time. He's coming for me. My heart is beating a primal drum rhythm now. I feel it pulse in my whole body. The aching, pulling throb of need.

My man is coming for me.

He's part warrior, part protector, and all glorious, sensual man.

He stops on a stair so that we are eye level for once. "You're really here." His eyes soften. "You look beautiful. I thought I was hallucinating when I heard him announce your name." His hand cups the back of my neck, and I see the intent in his eyes. I've seen it several times over the last few days.

"Everyone is watching us, Prince Markellan."

"Then let's give them something to see."

The moment his lips touch mine, I know I did the right thing by coming here. Even if it means being kissed by a prince in front of his entire kingdom. I drown in his spicy scent, melting into his kiss even as I hear the murmurs of the crowd.

He pulls back, and I see the reluctance to stop on his face. Placing my arm in his, he turns and addresses the crowd. "I am the consort of Miss Havisham," he says, and the murmurs grow louder. "Do me a favor and make a good impression on her this evening, everyone. My petition for marriage is not yet accepted. We are still in honeymoon."

I know my face is as red as the carpet we walk on as we finish the stairs and join his family at a table. Everyone is staring at me. They probably never expected their prince to find an uncultured American to bring home. One who is so plain among all the luxury around her.

Tara hugs me. "Brilliant. You were brilliant."

I pat my updo. "I couldn't have done it without you." I turn to Markellan. "Tara spent the day with me and a team of stylists. And Con taught me how to dance."

He shoots Con a look with daggers.

Con barely looks ruffled. "She asked for my help, Your Majesty. You ordered me to comply with her wishes."

His eyes are still narrowed, his chest still puffed up a bit, but he takes my hand tenderly. "Then let's dance."

The butterflies in my stomach are trying to get out of my skin before I puke up the last thing I ate, which was breakfast and a long time ago. I know I will trip, stumble, or step on his feet. Or all of the above. But he is waiting, one hand outstretched. He believes in me. I guess that will have to be enough for now. He won't let me fall even if I stumble.

"You take my breath away, Violet," he says as he pulls me in close.

This is nothing like dancing with my guard. Con kept a good foot of distance between us at all times. Markellan is grinding into me, making sure I can feel his erection despite how inappropriate he is being.

"This is the most done up I've ever been. I'm even wearing lipstick."

"I look forward to seeing that lipstick stain my cock, lamb," he whispers in my ear and suddenly I am moist and boneless. "This is your first ball, but I wonder how soon I can talk you into escaping. Or maybe ducking into a dark corner. I have a sudden need to know what you are wearing under that dress."

"We can't leave just yet."

"Why?" He groans into my neck. "I promise I will make it worth your while. Several times." Then he pulls back so I can see his face, and it's so serious given the way he's been carrying on. "I don't know if I can ever explain what it was like to hear your name, to see you like some kind of dream descending those stairs. Coming to me. My heart stopped in my chest, Violet. I've never seen anything so lovely as you facing your fears to be with me."

"There is something else I must do," I say. "Reach into your inside pocket."

His brow furrows, but he does as I ask and pulls out a satin ribbon I gave to Con earlier to sneak into his pocket. He blinks at the ribbon and swallows hard. "You have two days left," he reminds me, his voice filled with emotion. "You don't have to publicly bind yourself to me today."

"I don't need two days." I hold my hand up, and he grasps it in his. "Begin."

His breathing is shallow, and he looks so earnestly nervous that I feel better. He swallows hard but doesn't ask again if I'm sure. I told him I was and that is enough for him. He uses his other hand to wind the ritual satin around our wrists. "In the quiet space of your heart, do I live?" he asks, reciting the vows I just learned today while my hair was being burned into curls.

"There and the in-between," I answer. "May I be found in your love."

We both stare at our wrists, bound together, our hands clasped. "May it be ever thus," he says lowly, the gravel in his voice scrapes on the raw places of my heart.

Oh, I promised myself I wouldn't cry.

"May it be ever thus," I repeat, my knees nearly buckling.

His gaze goes dark and heated and I can see what he is thinking about. The things he wants to do to my body. The things he'll make me beg for as soon as we're alone. But even as we have this wordless conversation on the dance floor, a circle around us widens as the other dancers realize what is happening. He leans down, slanting his mouth over mine, and kisses me sweetly, gently. As he moves his mouth to my ear he whispers, "I'm going to make you come on my tongue."

I shiver, my mind going blank with lust for a moment.

And then there were pictures and hugging and dancing and eating and finally we arrive in the apartment, betrothed.

I did it. I'm really staying. I'm going to marry a prince.

He growls, a rumble of animal need, and pushes me into the wall. His body is rock hard against me, his hips grinding into the cradle of my thighs as he bunches my skirt up in his hands. "I need to be inside you."

I don't argue, just lock my arms around his neck and seal my mouth tightly to his. Then his hands move mine to the hem of my dress. "Hold this," he demands and drops to his knees, roughly moving my panties out of the way of his velvet tongue. He slides in deep and I cry out. I have to concentrate to hold my dress up. "You taste so fucking good. You were made for me. I was made to eat you up."

I come so fast it surprises us both, and he has to use his hand to hold my bottom so I don't fall. He turns me to the wall, his fingers taking the place of his tongue inside me. I feel his big, hard body behind me, pushing me. We're both still dressed, but hands roam over my body cupping, pinching and squeezing and his teeth bite and nip at my neck. He spreads my legs, and I feel the blunt head of his cock nudged against my pussy.

"Bend over." I bend and spread my legs wider, bracing myself against the wall. "Good girl."

I know this will be hard and fast. He needs it. I need it. I'm aching for it, my pussy clenching on emptiness while it waits for him.

He enters my pussy in one deep thrust. I feel impaled. Invaded as my body is shoved into the wall. He grabs my hair and pulls my head back and thrusts harder into my pussy. I can barely breathe.

"I need you too much," he says, his voice tight and harsh. "I didn't know it would be like this. Not even when I knew I had to have you. I didn't know. You make me feral, Violet." His teeth nip at the sensitive skin where my neck meets my shoulder, and I feel like I might pass out. "You. Are. Mine." He punctuates each word with a deep thrust, bottoming out inside me.

My senses are overwhelmed. He's rough, growling and groaning. My knees go weak and I am on the verge of collapsing on the floor, yet he surges inside me with another primal grunt. His body stiffens behind me and I feel him spilling into me, so hot and so deep. His cock pulses in my channel and triggers me into an orgasm so raw and stark I scream silently as my body convulses around him.

He holds me tight and pulls me up and into his arms as we both gasp for breath and slide to the floor, still in our formal wear.

As my pulse thunders in my ears, he moves behind me, curling his big body around me, the reassuring weight of him surrounding me.

"Did I hurt you? I was...rough."

"I like it when you're rough. I like it when you're slow and gentle. I like it when you're everything."

"Violet?"

"Hmmm?" I'm already drifting, floating on a soft cloud of bliss.

"I love you."

I stiffen, every muscle of my body tenses as if I've jumped into the coldest shower. My heart seizes, and my breath turns cold.

"Violet, what's wrong?" He turns me over, and I start sobbing. "Violet?" The concern on his face makes it worse, and I convulse, my body wracked with emotion I don't understand.

Markellan holds me through it and as the worst of it passes, he brings me to a sitting position and rocks me on the floor.

"I'm sorry. This is embarrassing," I say.

"Tell me what's wrong. Are you...you don't want me to love you...I thought..."

I clutch his arms. "That's not it, I swear. Of course I want you to love me. I swear. It's just that...nobody has said that to me in twenty years. I didn't know...I forgot what it feels like...You must think I'm crazy. I was just so young when they died. I know the nuns cared for me. And I've had friends. I just...I gave up thinking I would ever hear someone's heart speaking to mine."

He kisses the side of my head fiercely cupping the back of my neck firmly as he holds me to his chest. "I swear to you, there will never be another day in your life that you don't hear those words. You'll never question my feelings. I will always put you first. Always adore you. And when our children come, they will love you as much as I do."

I melt into him, into his heat. "I love you too, Markellan."

He pulls me across him and kisses me. I can still taste a trace of myself on his lips and it inflames my passion again.

I pull my mouth from his, dotting over the line of his jaw while I chant, "I love you," over and over. Somehow, we make it to the bed and I tell him again, using my body in ways I didn't know I could.

Epilogue

Markellan

Five Years Later

"Papa!" Our son Jaxen runs across the room when I enter, and I scoop up the blond monster with one arm and give him what he calls "kissickles" because my new beard tickles him when I give him kisses. "Hello, son. How is my little lad?"

"Mommy said I was such a good boy today that she forgot who my daddy was."

I laugh. "Oh, really."

My wife, my princess, my soul, crosses the room and just like always, when my eyes first see her, my heart skips a beat. She's beautiful, but there are shadows under her eyes. I pull my arm out dramatically from behind my back like I'm offering her flowers, only it's a bottle of ginger ale. "You look like you need this."

She smiles so big it breaks my heart. "Bless you." She takes the bottle from me and kisses me. "This is just what I need."

"I'm going to pretend you mean my kiss and not the soda."

"Your kiss is nice, too."

Her face is a little too pale, so I cup her cheek tenderly. "Bad today?"

"It will pass."

"Maybe Mommy needs some kissickles too. Mommy likes the kisses that tickle, doesn't she?"

She blushes, even after all this time. But I don't let it fool me. She's the one who asked me to grow the beard. She definitely likes the kissickles.

Jaxen pulls us both to the couch talking about some game that makes him so happy that has pixelated squares and a heavy merchandising budget. After his lengthy explanation, we sit him between us for a very important talk.

Violet takes the medallion out of her pocket and hands it to me. I kiss her hand as I take it.

"Son, we need to talk."

"What is it, Papa?"

I hold up the medallion. "Do you know what this is?"

He nods. "It's the coin Mommy carries everywhere."

"That's right. Daddy gave Mommy the coin when she was a little girl and she was scared. Do you know who gave Daddy the coin?"

"Grandpapa King in Heaven."

"That's right. He gave it to Daddy when I was about your age. Told me it was very important to him, but he wanted me to have it so I would always feel him with me. A few years later, he went to Heaven, but I always remembered him. And I gave it to Mommy so she would always remember me."

She strokes his hair. "And now, we want you to have it. And keep it with you always. So you always know how much we love you."

He takes it reverently. Like we just gave him Excalibur. Violet looks a little bit like I felt the day I gave it up. It still sucks to do the right thing sometimes. At least she won't have to wait for twenty years to see it again.

"There's something else, big boy," she says to him. She takes his hand and puts it over her stomach. "You're going to be a big brother."

"Me?" he asks. "You have a baby in your tummy?"

We've explained to him the basics of babies before, as it is the custom of Kentigen to bring children up knowing and understanding such things. Not more than he can handle, but enough that he knows babies are made with love and grow inside mommies until they come out.

We continue to talk to him about what it might be like to be a big brother. The perks and the big boy responsibilities and when we finally get him to sleep, my wife looks ready to pass out.

"Come," I say, holding my hand out and then leading her into the bathroom where I draw her a bath, feed her crackers and ginger ale, and wash her back.

"When we get out of this tub, I will give you a nice, long massage."

She looks over her shoulder at me. "That is the same line you told me twelve weeks ago that got me into this mess."

I put my hand over her stomach possessively. "You didn't complain about it that night."

She covers my hand with hers. "I'm so happy right now. Even though I might throw up."

Later, when the worst of her nausea has passed, I roll toward her on our bed, nestling into her, my arm around her hips, drawing her tight into the shelter of my body, spooning up against her back.

She sighs sweetly, and it stirs something deep inside me. My love for her just gets deeper every day.

My cock, now rubbing against her ass, grows harder, as always, and a drop of pre-cum seeps from the tip. I slowly push into her, sliding into Heaven. I'm in no hurry. Tonight I want to go slow. Cherish her. Softly, carefully, I arch my hips driving forward until I am inside her as far as I can go, my balls pressed against the wet entrance to her pussy. I stay there, in her tight, wet sheath, and feel her stretching around me.

"You're amazing," I tell her as my cock twitches involuntarily inside her.

I slide out gently, then back in again, the smell of our sex filling the room in a scent no rare flower of Kentigen can match for an aphrodisiac.

Again, I slide out and in, enjoying the exquisite friction between us, taking in the smell of her hair and the softness of her skin, feeling her hand brush against mine.

She turns her head to me so I lean forward and kiss her, our tongues entwining. She moans softly as I begin to thrust into her pussy again, my cock sliding in and out with long, insistent strokes, faster and faster.

Her hand grabs mine and pulls it to a breast, pushing my fingers across the surface and over her nipple, which hardens under our collective touch.

Thrusting my cock in deep strokes, I push one of her hands down onto her pussy and we both play with her clit together.

"That's it, love. Touch yourself. I love it when you play with your pussy."

I can feel the cum rising in my balls, threatening my climax already. I groan, not ready for it to end, yet unable to stop the increase of speed and depth of my thrusts, pressing our hands into her pussy. She tenses and holds her breath, a signal I've come to know. She's right there.

"Yes, angel. Come all over my cock." She squeezes her thighs together, and her hips make sharp little jerks in time with her quiet little cries, her tight pussy contracting hard around my cock, milking me.

I can't hold back any longer. With a primal moan, cum surges through my cock and deep inside of her, the heat spreading through and around us both, my hips banging in shaking spasms. She comes again, tightening around me, draining every last drop from me.

We stay entwined, neither of us ready for me to pull out, until sleep takes us both. My dreams are never as good as my reality now. Not since we found each other again. But they are sweet anyway.

About the Author

Brill Harper is a pseudonym. Like...a secret identity. By day she's Clark Kent, writing romance books for young adults and grownups. By night, she's Brill Harper writing unfailingly filthy yet super sweet books that would make her alter ego blush.

Brill like Alpha heroes with an ooey-gooey heart when they fall in love. She calls them Alphamallows.

Visit Brill on her website: https://brillharper.com/

Get VIP early access status and more: https://reamstories.com/brillharper

Join Brill on: Facebook[1]

---

1. https://www.facebook.com/Brill-Harper-1931520800417566/

Also by Brill Harper

Blue Collar Bad Boys
Bounced: A Blue Collar Bad Boys Book
Nailed: A Blue Collar Bad Boys Book
Drilled: A Blue Collar Bad Boys Book
Wrecked: A Blue Collar Bad Boys Book
Laid: A Blue Collar Bad Boys Book
Tagged
Plowed
Bucked: A Blue Collar Bad Boys Book
Banged: A Blue Collar Bad Boys Book
Tapped: A Blue Collar Bad Boy Book

It's Complicated
All Together
All at Once

Love in Brazen Bay
Wrong Number Text
The Right Stuff
So Wrong It's Right

Don't Get Me Wrong

Standalone
Dirty Jobs: a Blue Collar Bad Boys Collection
Notch on His Bedpost
Honeymoon With The Prince: A Royal Romance
Good Girl

Watch for more at https://brillharper.com.